Denton Jaques Snider

Clarence

A drama

Denton Jaques Snider

Clarence
A drama

ISBN/EAN: 9783337057015

Printed in Europe, USA, Canada, Australia, Japan

Cover: Foto ©Andreas Hilbeck / pixelio.de

More available books at **www.hansebooks.com**

CLARENCE,

A Drama in Three Acts.

BY D. J. SNIDER.

DRAMATIS PERSONNÆ:

—————•·•·•—————

COL. DE HARRISON.

CLARA, *his daughter.*

EDWARD, *her cousin.*

JEAN D'ORVILLE.

CLARENCE.

THE CAPTAIN.

HARWOOD.

SERGEANT.

HODDLE.

BUMBLE.

A COUNTRYMAN.

FOLLOWERS OF THE CAPTAIN,

PLANTERS.

—————•·•·•—————

ERRATA.

On page 28, line 38, read, "I have *it* now," instead of "I have *in* now."

On page 31, line 9 of Scene Fourth, read, "So fair a face that I do rue my choice," instead of "So fair a face that I do *me* rue my choice."

CLARENCE.

ACT I.

Clara, *sola.*

Once more with ancient joy the fragrant air,
Which softly rests among these trees, I breathe,
And in this grove, o'erarched with mighty limbs,
And roofed with thickly woven twigs and leaves
Ceaselessly trembling in the evening wind,
And darting fitful glimmers 'neath the moon,
I take my old habitual walk of youth.
This wood sits like a crown upon the plain,
And in its umbrage sweet of quiet holds
The garden and the mansion of my father.
My bosom swells to see these dear old forms
Rising so grandly to the starry cope:
Methinks ye seem to recognize me, too,
With nodding heads and merry, fluttering leaves,
The happy child that gamboled at your feet.
Here, here were spent my days of golden dreams,
Ere I had felt the tender pang of love,
Or heard the tread of swiftly-stepping hours.
Stretch forth your arms, ye mighty oaks of eld,
Embrace the mossy roof in tender curves
That fondly hover o'er the sacred pile,
As if to shield it from the outer world.
To you a debt of gratitude is due,
For ye were ever friendly to my race.
My fathers—ye have seen and known them all;
Each season ye have spread your lofty tents
Of moving green for them to rest beneath,   [*garden.*
And on your own heads fell the burning ray. *Passes into the*
These many colored rows and blooming paths
Call, too, my childhood back, its hours of joy;
Here is the flower bed which I called mine,
Here is the lily which I nursed to growth.
Alas! the one, unweeded, tells the tale
Of my long abscence and its own neglect;

The other scarce can raise its sickly face
Above the fierce and envious grass around.
Unfeeling 'twas to leave you thus alone !
Sweet little children of the soil, ye speak
Of years that never shall be mine again.   *Passes out.*
Where have I been ?   Those years how have I passed ?
My spirit wanders to the distant hills
Whence I have just arrived, and lingers there
On many a scene of loveliness and joy.
O dear New England ! thou art great and fair !
How beautiful thy mountains and thy vales !
But Nature there puts on not robes so gay
And bright as in my own beloved South.
Upon this spot would I contented die,
Nor envy Northern beauty, greatness, worth,
If one fair spirit of that clime were here
To share with me this happy dwelling place.
Yes, him I grudge the land of ice and snow :
That noble form and fiery, daring soul
Belong not there ; within this bower here
Should be his home ; our double life were thus
A flowing stream, a swelling sea of love :
It were a happiness too deep for thought.
Oh ! God ! wherefore thy decree so harsh !
Oh ! Earth ! why hast thou cast thyself between
And torn our hands apart, our hearts asunder !
But hush !   I must be calm ; there is no hope.
He knows not of my love, or else it scorns,
And thus my first affection, like the rose,
Which, putting forth its earliest, fairest bud,
At heart is eaten by the cankerous worm
Ere it unfolds its leaves unto the sun,
And falls despairing to the ground and dies :
So, too, my love is bitten and destroyed
Before the fruit of wedlock is mature.
Its corpse I must entomb, and in its stead
Remains my aged father ;—fair return
It is, I deem ;—him shall I nurse and love,
Till Death shall steal his form from my embrace.
Such is my duty and such is my desire ;
Thus solace may I find by giving it.
The dear old man ! he wept to see his child,
And now his child should see him weep no more.
Here, then, I willing take the virgin vow
To banish the sweet thought of family,
The mystic bond of man's and woman's love,

To live encloistered with this single aim—
To smooth my father's pathway to the grave.

SCENE SECOND.—*Boats full of men,* CLARENCE *as pilot.*
CAPTAIN.

Capt. I grow impatient; is the landing near?
Clar. A few more lusty strokes and we are there.
Capt. Strike fast! I cannot wait; my body frets,
And like a roweled charger rears with pain;
I feel the sword hilt burning in my grasp;
My smothered nature struggles for the work
Of death, as for her vital atmosphere.
Clar. Already we are in the little bay
Where we shall hide the birth of our emprise;
This dark recess surrounded by the hills,
O'erspread with woods and woven thickets deep,
Secures us from th' approach and gaze of man,
And can betray no word by us here spoken.
Capt. Good Clarence, here I take thy faithful hand;
Thy trust was great; thou hast it well fulfilled
In bringing us to this most fitting place.
Clar. I had to pray to thy unwillingness.
Capt. But now I'm glad I granted thy request,
And such confession carries double thanks.
Clar. Peace! Peace! Heave too, my boys! This is the spot
Which first of Southern soil dares you receive
Into its bosom deep of shade and quietude.
Followers. Hail!
Capt. Ha? 'tis the infernal world! Accursed shore,
Manured with the lives and souls of men!
The hellish element I smell already.
Clar. Our need is action now, speech not at all.
Distant denunciation of the wrong
Beyond the stroke of danger was our trade;
Here wordy weapons will no more avail.
Capt. Do not prescribe the compass of my speech:
When I have failed or faltered in the deed
Is season for reproof.
Fols.   Hail! ho! the land!
Capt. The land long sought! that which we shall redeem
Or redden with its own foul dragon blood.
1 Fol. Hurrah for Liberty!
All. Hurrah?   [*on the bayonet of a musket.*
2 Fol. Her cap must ever be a cartridge box. *Raises a cartridge box*

All. Hurrah ?

Clar. Another pull ! Gruffly she scours the sand.
  Leap to the shore !

Capt.   Revenge is nigh at hand. *Jumps ashore.*
  The first to break this soil, I shall be last
  To print my tracks reversed upon its face ;
  Its thirsty pores shall drink my blood like rain
  Ere it beholds my flight. *Strikes his sword into the ground.*
                    Thus shall this land,
  With war and desolation rent and pierced,
  Wail out in bitter, late acknowledgement
  That Man is Man, whate'er may be his race,
  Whate'er the tint that God paints on his skin.
  Disperse now to the wood and seek the shade ; *To his folls.*
  Rest there your wearied limbs from heavy toil,
  You've pulled for many a league the sea-dividing oar,
  And we, your chosen leader in this raid,
  Shall find another spot not far away ;
  We too need sorely counsel and repose.

Scene Third.—*The mansion of* De Harrison.

Enter Col. De Harrison.

A new star hath risen on my life,
Scattering joy and peace along its course,
Dispelling gloom with fair and radiant face :
My only daughter, whom I have not seen
Since she has shorn her girlish curls of gold,
And donned the lengthened dress of womanhood,
Returns now to the bosom of her father,
A full blown flower of fairest dye,
To deck the way of his descending years.
My home has now become a home indeed !
E'en the quick blood of youthful wantonness
Runs tingling through my veins, and all my limbs,
Beaten so long with strokes of gout and age,
Move with the new-born ease of little babes.
A single sadness darkly crapes my soul ;
She calls forth from the tomb an image dear,
A form forever lost to me and her,
My wife, her mother ; whom I have bewept
Till age has slipped upon me unawares :
Who could but reproduce herself and die.
This dearly purchased blossom hath now bloomed,
And shows the very picture of its race ;

The easy movement and the gentle grace,
The modest, coy, yet all-subduing glance,
An eye that melts the very stones to love,
That fragile form, are all her mother's gifts,
The fairest heritage e'er left a maid ;
But Nature not alone has spent its bounty
To decorate her person with its wealth ;
The nobler qualities of cultured worth,
The union bright of intellect and feeling,
The very diamond in the crown of woman,
Are hers ; for this I parted from her youth,
And sent her to the best of Northern schools
To be my worthy representative,
And heir to my estate and ancient name.
But long she must not here remain and hide
Her beauty and desert within these walls ;
A dear companion worthy of her house,
And of her love, must be the next choice boon,
That caps the highest summit of our bliss—
Here comes Jean.   *Enter Jean D' Orville.*
                    Son of my dearest friend
And worthiest neighbor, welcome to my abode !
Hither thy visits turn not oft of late.

Jean. Too oft, by once, at least, I've passed your house.
Col. Hast thou by any person here been wronged ?
Jean. Yea ; I might say I have been foully robbed.
Col. Name the offender, on the spot he suffers.
Jean. The theft is not of gold or sensuous stuff,
    Nor is the doer conscious of the deed.
Col. Surely, thou art not well to-day, Jean.
Jean. In truth, much cause have I to be not well.
Col. I traced some illness in thy haggard eyes,
    That erst so full of fire defied the world.
Jean. But now, a glance has vanquished all their might.
Col. Beneath thy random speech some foul disease
    Doth seem to lurk and carry off thy wits.
Jean. My mind is not at home, but gone astray ;
    Has found a new heart and will not return.
Col. What is thy ailment ? Enter, rest thyself.
Jean. 'Tis a complaint most common to young men,
    Though ne'er before my soul hath felt its pangs.
Col. Tell me, I pray, hast thou been long thus ill ?
Jean. Since yesterday. The attack was sudden, deep,
    A flash it came and left a festering wound,
    Which feasts upon my spirit and my flesh.
Col. What did the doctor say ? Has he been called ?

Jean. Alas! it yields not to the assaults of physic.

Col. 'Tis pitiful! can I do aught for thee?

Jean. The magic word to work my cure thou hast.

Col The darkness of thy speech bewilders me;
That robbery of which thou speak'st was strange;
More strange the sickness which I am to cure.

Jean. Hast thou ne'er heard of the arrowed god
Nor felt his shaft in thy warm youthful days?
Yestreen at dusk along this field I roamed;
Within this garden here, and in the wood,
I saw an angel walking to and fro,
Gathering flowers and humming some soft ditty,
A humming-bird collecting dainty sweets.
A smile was always sporting o'er her face,
The messenger of happiness within;
And ever and anon she spoke aloud
To some spirit-shape that viewless hovered o'er.
Then passing out her grot she threw a glance
That caused my heart to beat against his walls,
As if he would break out his prison-cell,
To run and greet his bright deliverer.
Since then I have been faint and deathly sick,
My lonely sighs have filled the day and night,
Nor can I charm repose with rosy wings,
To come and perch upon my feverish brow.

Col. Let thy address be plain and to the point.

Jean. I shall so speak that in my very words
The meaning will as clearly be reflected,
As the face that looks upon the crystal brook.
It is thy daughter that hath stolen my mind;
It flies to her and will not stay by me;
Nought can I see but her bright darting form,
Which haunts the plastic air where'er I turn.
This is the malady which thou can'st cure,
By thy consenting voice, and *thou* alone.
O, reach to me I pray, thy daughter's hand,
And join in promise now her soul to mine!

Col. Jean, thee have I deemed a noble youth,
Among our cavaliers thou hast no peer.
Most willingly I grant my full consent,
And e'en will help thee with a kindly word.
But mark! I shall not force my daughter's choice;
No right have I to cast her future life
Into my moulds against her will; no right
Have I to give away her happiness,
Which is her dower granted at her birth.

Go, the decision she alone can give,
With her consent, already thou hast mine.

SCENE FOURTH.—*A wood and a camp in the same.*

Enter SERGEANT *and* HODDLE.

Ser. Hoddle, here! the Captain wants a fire.
Hod. Then let him make it and not look to me.
Ser. What's that? I hope I understood thee not.
Hod. Thy hope is run aground, I shall not stir.
Ser. Good Hoddle, go, else thou mayest make me wroth!
Hod. Thy wrath has power over me no longer.
Ser. Thou saucy cur! dost thou bemock my words—
Hod. We are all equal now, that's our motto.
Ser. And disobey the Captain's orders too?
Hod. Am I not free as you or any other man?
  Can I not have my will, control myself?
  Wherefore should anybody say to me:
  "Hoddle, do thus, and thus," or "thou shalt not;"
  Henceforth I'll have my rights, I'll serve no more.
Ser. What thought rebellious surges in thy breast,
  And threatens to submerge authority?
Hod. Ah! wherefore came we o'er the furious sea,
  And risked our lives upon the briny deep;
  It was to free the bondsman of his chains,
  And bring a light unto his darkened mind.
  Therefore, most willingly I joined this band
  To aid the holy work it undertook.
  But first I swear to liberate myself,
  And break the shackles of another's will,
  Which now encompass me and weigh me down.

Enters CAPTAIN.

Capt. What, Hoddle, ho! why tarriest thou so long—
  Sergeant, hast thou delivered my commands?
Ser. To thy summons he refused obedience,
  And grandly talked of freedom and of rights,
  From him by us most wrongfully withheld,
  Which he henceforth would have in spite of us;
  And thus he spake with speech most fair yet false,
  Profaning sacred words with slavish tongue.
Capt. The knave, the villain! he too, will seek his rights,
  And nip the budding promise of our work;
  Meanwhile, the sable slave toils on in death,
  And prays in vain for a deliverer.
  I'll give a lesson to his mutinous tongue,   [*him.*

	And teach a right he ought to've known e'er this. *Striking*
Hod.	Oh, my poor back, still swollen with the blows
	Of yesterday, and ridged in painful welts!
	Spare, spare, I pray! O spare thy strokes! I'll go,
	I'll go, and never disobey again.
Capt.	Enough! Now, Sergeant, take him at his word. *Exit Capt.*
Ser.	Good Hoddle, I have always been thy friend;
	Deeply it grieves my soul to see thee punished,
	More deeply still, to know that thou deserved'st it.
	Now go to yonder thicket and gather leaves
	And little twigs to set the fire ablaze;
	Thou hast been in the army, so thou say'st:
	This is the soldier's way to cook his supper.
Hod.	Nothing is known to thee of soldiers' ways.
Ser.	'Tis true, I never fired a gun; yet know
	That God is with the right, weak though it be—
	But to proceed. If thou wilt pass yon farm-house,
	And slyly snatch a fowl both fat and young,
	To be served up before the Captain here,
	It will go far to pacify his ire,
	And to restore thee to thy former favor.
	I too, shall lend my tongue to help thy suit.
	If thou wilt fetch a second fatted capon.
Hod.	Thy piety is followed by a thief,
	And will be overtaken soon methinks.
Ser.	A little wrong wont hurt when 'tis for right,
	For wrong is right if it is done for right;
	To pat the Devil's shoulder in God's name,
	Is held an ancient Christian privilege.
	But I must bring this prating to a close,
	Go, do the errand which I've mentioned;
	Yet mark, my boy, thine eye keep outward turned,
	See all, yet do not let thyself be seen,
	Lest our success perchance, ourselves may perish,
	E'er we have set the fiery ball in motion.
	There are some people in this neighborhood,
	Who fain would prick the bubble but dare not touch
	The bombshell. Now be shy, my boy, be shy. *Exit.*
Hod.	Whipped like a dog, treated like a slave;
	And yet they say they came to free the slave;
	I took their words for true, upon my back
	Are stamped in blood the marks of foolish trust;
	An inconsistency that frightens Hell!
	Had I the rooting jaw, the flattened nose,
	The hard laniferous pate, I would have friends
	And sympathy; but now I am o'erborne

By hate of men, who cherish in their breasts
A prejudice 'gainst the Caucasian tint,
And so I have the glorious privilege of a drudge—
I must be off now, else my bleeding back
Will weep afresh its rueful tears of blood.

———

SCENE FIFTH.—FOLLOWERS *in Camp*, BUMBLE.

Bum. Oh, Heaven! wretched me! I am a mighty sinner.
1 Fol. What's the matter, Bumble?
Bum. I wish I was at home.
1 Fol. Cursed be that word till the job is done.
2 Fol. You rue your coming hither, then?
Bum. O, for the comforts of a mother's care!
3 Fol. He cannot do without his mother yet.
2 Fol. Well, then, we shall have to wean him.
Bum. This chilly dampness is killing me.
1 Fol. Then you'll die the death of a martyr to the cause.
2 Fol. A glorious death; that's what we all are seeking.
Bum. I sought it in the distance, but in the distance
I want it to stay.   Near by it looks too ugly.
1 Fol. Your words are outrageously profane, sir.
2 Fol. And disrespectful to this noble enterprise.
3 Fol. He is unworthy of our lofty purpose.
Bum. I see no good which can result from this mad chase.
1 Fol. Are we not doing God's will?
Bum. It may be His, it is not mine.
2 Fol. And fighting for the Right.
Bum. Right; a thing of fancy, nobody ever saw it.
3 Fol. Men never bled in a holier cause.
Bum. It has not come to bleeding yet, and I hope it won't.
All. Coward! coward.
1 Fol. Thy spoils should be a rope and limb.
All. A rope! a rope!
2 Fol. We'll hiss the traitor out of camp.
All. Traitor! traitor!
3 Fol. The better plan is to throw the wretch into the sea.
All. So be it.   Huzzah! To the sea with him!

[*Enter* CLARENCE.]

Clar. Silence! what means this noise, and riot here
Which warns the foe of his approaching hour?
3 Fol. Tear off the honest armor from his side.
All. Away with him, away!
Clar. Stop! are ye mad?   Hold, here, unhand that man!
Know ye the penalty of this rash act?
An earthquake now is rumbling 'neath your feet,

O, fools! and yet ye fight among yourselves.
Wherefore this sudden frenzy 'gainst your comrade?

1 Fol. No, no, he's not of us; we own him not.

2 Fol. He spoke most vilely of our sacred cause,
And slandered us, to whom it is most dear;
He will go home, play coward, traitor to the Right.

Clar. Dost thou not see the downy chin of youth,
And read excuse therein for every word?

2 Fol. Not we, his own free-will brought him along.

Clar. His was the impulse of a noble soul
To help a captive race to cleave its fetters.

2 Fol. Why does he fly before the work is done?

Clar. Young are his bones, by hardship yet unsteeled,
And hence he crouches 'neath the frown of danger.

3 Fol. Salt water baths are said to cure weak knees.

All. Good, good, 'tis true.

Bum. You all will need to take a bath ere long.

1 Fol. Hush, forked tongue!

All.   Seize him! Rush to the shore.

Clar. Hold, hold, I say! Be quiet while I speak.
This wrangling is the dire destructive Hell,
Which swallows up yourselves and all your hopes.
Endure a word for this young man, I ask.
He laid foul epithets upon our cause;
Such is the charge. It was the first impatience
At Fortune's halting gait, methinks; no more.
I might feel thus myself and use vile words;
But the long trial of my age doth teach
That oft between the plan and the fulfillment,
There lies an arduous hill, and this the youth
Unstable and untried, doth tire in climbing;
For in the glow of the conceiving thought
Light Phantasy that wings the minds of youth,
May overlook this rugged interval.
The warm begetting of our dear device
At first we feel, and then at once we see
The bright and happy end, but the rough tract
Which lies between and constitutes the deed,
Remains to us unknown and unexplored.

1 Fol. I fear his heart is not with us, else why
Should he with a reviling tongue berate
Our holy undertaking, for whose sake
We're lying here along this dreary coast
Like shipwrecked strangers on an ocean isle.

2 Fol. We of this entire nation steeped in sin
Are come to meet the fiend on his own ground;

And must we listen to reproaches now,
Thrown out by one of our own number, too ?

Clar. In firm devotion to our worthy aim
And hatred to the demon of this soil,
No one shall me surpass ; my zeal is known :
Who left at home a life of ease and wealth?
Who steered you hither through the wayless deep ?
But on my merits I shall not descant :
O, cease this ugly rancor and this strife
Which mars the peace and holiness—
Wherein our boasts are loud—of our good work.
Wait but a few short hours, ye then will have
A nobler prey at which ye may direct
All your superfluous shafts of rage and valor.
Our enemies are near, these their domains ;
Here are the people whom we came to slay,
Here are the bondsmen whom we came to free,
Therefore, lay up your strength for other scenes,
For ye will need it all.   Come with me, Bumble.   *Exeunt.*

SCENE SIXTH.—*Enter* CLARENCE *and* CAPTAIN.

Capt. I have forgotten ; Clarence, where's the boat,
Which cut so bravely through the salty spray,
And bore us boldly here in its embrace,
Fighting the traitorous wave at every move ?
Hast thou disposed of it in any way?

Clar. Yonder it lies, moored safely on the beach,
Beneath the low o'erhanging foliage,
That lines the ocean with a verdant span,
And views itself in every passing billow ;
This secret spot conceals the craft which thus
May serve us well again in time of need.

Capt. I shall not have it so, for then there comes
A hope that we can flee and still be safe,
And this may foil our noble enterprise.
The foolish thought of a secure retreat
Has often brought defeat upon great armies,
Which else held surest victory in their grasp ;
And so this boat, peacefully rocking here,
May make us cowards in the hour of strife,
When the decision trembles in the scale.
We must be brave ; Despair shall make us brave.
Straightway I'll go and cut the hawsers loose,
And give it to the waves to roll away

Beyond the reach of our retreating steps.   *Exit.*

Clar. [*Solus*].   'Tis well, perhaps, I scarce shall need it more ;
It brought me safely hither o'er the deep ;
Its work for me is done, forever done,
For a return lies not within my plans.
Security for her is now the thought
Which thrills and stirs to action every nerve ;
To save her kindred from the bloody knife,
Herself from poverty and orphanage,
T'avert the dreadful strife of warring men,
Which else might come within her very door,
I joined this headstrong band and hither came,
When I had learned their first attack aimed here.
I feigned the garb of faithfulness and zeal,
Their cause not to betray, but her preserve.
O, if the outcome tally with my hope,
And I restore her fortune and her life,
'Twill be a token of my burning love
Whose mute appeal her heart can not resist,
Then shall I kneel and look into her face
And tell the story of my adventurous deed,
Then shall I press her tender hand in mine
Nor ever pass beyond her radiant glance.
O, brightest constellation of the South !
While thou didst move within our wintry sphere,
The Heavens glowed with a refulgent splendor,
And all the land adored pure Beauty's ray.
Oft have I gazed upon thy beaming face
And worshipped thee within my deepest soul,
And felt transfigured at thy heavenly look.
But hold ! my fancy runs before and steals
The shining prize ere it is reached in deed !
How shall I find her home ?   How let her know
Mine own intent, the danger hanging o'er ?
What envious mountains rise to thwart my hopes !
For ah ! my passion is to her unknown,
This act must prove its fervor and its depth.
In such conjuncture so it seemeth best :
Our troop must send a spy to note the land,
And seek the fittest point to fire the train ;
For this nice service I shall volunteer,
And none, methinks, can stand against my claim,
Because I was of late the chosen guide
To cut a road upon the pathless main.
Dispatched again and having free my way,
Soon shall I find the happy hidden spot,
Which holds the fairest rose of this bright clime.

ACT. II.

SCENE FIRST—*DeHarrison's Mansion.*

Enter COL. DEHARRISON *and* CLARA.

Col. My daughter, welcome to thy ancient home,
Which, forest-girt, sits lonely 'mong these hills;
Thy face shall light anew its darkened halls,
And cause to sprout afresh its mossy grandeur;
Or has thy absence blotted out these charms?

Cl. No, father, I deserve not e'en a slight reproach,
For ever, when I've wandered far away,
This mansion rose within my mind, and shone
The star of Hope to which my journey bent;
And 'round the aged form within these walls,
Have gathered all the wishes of my life.

Col. O, Love, thy sea has ne'er been sounded yet,
Nor have the depths of woman's heart been reached!
Be queen, my daughter, of this fair abode;
'Tis all the rank I can confer on thee.

Cl. Enough; I would not change this simple crown,
Which gives me household rule and care of thee,
For all the thrones that sway the Eastern world.

Col. This is the picture of thy mother's mind,
To be the hidden jewel of her home,
Nor seek the profane gazes of the world.
O, since that fair and early bloom was cut,
And withered 'neath the stroke of mowing Death,
Joy, with her many-colored fragrant wings,
From whose light movement blessings strew the earth,
Has flown beyond the journey of my life,
Nor shaken once her pinions o'er my head.

Cl. O Father! let me be that joy to thee!
Thy silvered crown I'll deck with roses,
The emblem bright of thy peace-anchored soul;
I'll soothe thy wearied spirit with my song,
And lean o'er thee to fight off vampire care,
Whose dainty food's the minds of sad, unhappy men;
And ne'er shall sorrow with her dark-veiled face
Again approach thy couch of balmy rest.

Col. O God! the image of my sainted bride
Has now returned from her sojourn above,
To cheer me in the lengthening shade of life.

Cl.   I see, thy thoughts are in the grassy grave,
      Whose long white finger points above the yews
      That guard the peopled mounds of yonder churchyard,
      And join their weeping limbs to shade the sod.
      Tell me, I pray, of my departed mother.
      I know not what it is to have a mother;
      That pious word whose might commands the founts
      Which wash in brine the cheeks of human kind,
      Ne'er sweetened with its tender sound my breath.
      Tell me her ways, her qualities of mind;
      Show me the dress which she was wont to wear,
      The hat that won thy youthful fantasy;
      Lisp but the accent of her daily speech,
      And I will catch the color of its tone;
      I'll so put on her character and life,
      That thou shalt say, My mother is not dead;
      Her death and burial were a hideous dream.

Col.   Be thine own self, it is enough for me;
      To make such change would be a changeless change.
      It pains yet pleases me to speak of her,
      Whom once my youth led to the wreathed altar,
      More blooming than the flowers that loosely hung
      With contrast sweet among her glossy tresses.
      Then were our lives as gladsome as the birds
      That greet the first warm peep of merry Spring,
      Warbling out their hearts sitting in the sun.
      But ah! fell winter, hurried ere his time;
      He froze that bursting rose of womanhood,
      And bleached my locks before the snows of Age
      Had fallen on my sorrow-wrinkled brow.
      O! well I recollect the woful tide:
      December month had chilled our sunny clime,
      Rough Boreas struck us with his frosty wings,
      And snatched away the spirit of thy mother.
      Deep in the smallest hour of night it was,
      I raised thee o'er her bed within my arms,
      To catch her parting glance and final blessing;
      She oped her dying eyes, on thee she cast
      One long, sad, loving look, then fell asleep.

Cl.   That dark time comes to me the primal link
      Wherewith my memory starts the chain of life;
      Before that hour I know nought of myself.
      The wistful, farewell-look I still can see;
      And this alone, remains to me of her;
      A keepsake which Time can not steal or dim.

Col.   How thou grew'st up the fairest of thy comrades,

The idol of the slaves, the favorite
Of all the neighborhood and town,
I tell thee not. And hence this narrow sphere
Should not restrain thy universal gifts,
But thou should'st see the world and know the world,
And nought in chance should fail to have thee called
The worthy daughter of DeHarrison.
Now thou art come from thy long pilgrimage
Of travel, study, culture, toilsome ways,   •
To shower all thy wealth upon my head ;
Be mistress then of these ancestral halls,
Wherein thy queenly mother erst did reign.

Col. How oft have I looked to this happy time !
When far away among white crested hills,
Or riding on old ocean's foam-crowned head,
This sweet, sweet hour was filling all my thoughts.
Here is the long-watched goal, here are the walls,
Beyond whose bounds ambition stretches not.

Col. But not forever here with me alone thou'dst dwell ?

Cl. Such is the sealed purpose of my life.

Col. Thy will runs counter to the grain of nature ;
'Tis not the daughter's destiny to spend
Her maiden bloom upon her father's path.

Cl. Mine let it be. I shall not rue my course.

Col. Youth needs a youthful mate for its embrace.

Cl. Youth needs gray hairs to calm its raging blood.

Col. Families perish that families arise ;
The filial bond Time soonest rends in twain ;
And so thy love to me must be transferred.

Cl. You seem to hint at aught remote and dark.
Veil not thy meaning's features from my gaze,
For thought is worthy of a shining garb ;
Address the comprehension of a maid.

Col. Thy schooled wit appears not now at home,
Have twenty summers warmed thy generous heart,
And not brought forth a single germ of love ?
I know the heat of youth, our Southern blood ;
The seal of this hot clime still stamps thy brow ;
Speak ! what thou art it is no shame to be.

Cl. Go to, have I not said ? Yes, *thee* I love.

Col. Such prevarication is a whit unkind ;
It is a charge 'gainst me of foul mistrust ;
Thy love to *me* is known, I meant it not.

Cl. O, must I then disrobe my secret soul,
And set its nakedness before thy eyes ?
Its chastity doth shrink beneath a look,

And tries to hide within its own dark self.
I've told the single purpose of my bosom,
To ease for thee the strokes of smiting age,
What else lies hidden there I will forget.
The heart was buried deep within the breast
To keep more safely all its golden treasures;
Break not into this holy shrine I pray,
Where lie my soul's most sacred offerings.

Col.   Not for the world, my dear; thy will is thine;
But those entreaties and that traitorous blush,
The secret implication of thy speech,
Have darkly answered all my questionings.
Yet in what safer hiding-place think'st thou,
Could be concealed the secret of thy life,
Than in the breast of him that gave thee life?

Cl.   Thou can'st command my thoughts, my hopes, myself;
Forgive, my duty would I not deny.

Col.   With that stern voice thee shall I never call.
The low, sweet note of tenderness and love
Alone, will woo thine ear within these halls.
I fain would know who won this noble prize,
For which the world might run in envious games;
What pictured form of man reflects itself
Upon the crystal clearness of thy heart?
O may it be as pure as its surroundings,
A likeness fair in golden frame of love.   [*breast.*

Cl.   Thou art the monarch sole of all this realm;   *Points at her*
Thee there enthroned no rival can depose.

Col.   It is then void; fill up its emptiness.
Paternal love agrees with conjugal;
And I would deem thee not a daughter lost,
But e'en thy spouse a son to me new-born.
It grieves my mind to think thy future lot,
To see thee resting on an aged trunk,
Whose swift decay of heart doth near the bark,
Whose bending top looks down and threats the grave.
O, seek while it is time a firmer stock.

Cl.   The verdant ivy hugs the fallen oak.
Reposing e'en in Death upon his breast,
And twines green wreathes around her spouse's corpse.

Col.   Dumb nature shows us what we ought to shun.
How rough my bed of death the thought would make,
Of dragging down a living heart into the tomb!
Find speedy prop to hold thy fragile frame.

Cl.   O, heavy burden of two-faced commands!
O, will that longs to do and not to do!

My head is cleft, my brain 's the seat of war,
And Thought is trying to destroy itself!
T'obey and disobey are now alike:
O Duty, thou deservest not thy fame,
For oft thou art a cheat and double-tongued;
Thy fickle breath now bids me stay with father,
Then lightly whispers: Follow his behest—   *Turns to him.*
Thy will is *mine;* obedience is my vow.
Hast thou yet found the sharer of my lot?

Col. Know once again, thine own free will must choose;
'Tis mere suggestion, no command I give.
A youth of noble port and gallant mien
I know; of gentle ancestry and name,
And disposition martial, proud and brave,
Yet tender in his feelings as a child;
Warm-hearted, chivalrous and hospitable:
Perchance at times a little choleric,
For in his veins the blood doth course as swift,
As pure as e'er throbbed through a Southern heart.
Wealth too, has oped to him her golden purse,
And poverty can never cross his sill.
Hast thou yet seen our neighbor D'Orville's son?

Cl. Whom? What's the name? D'Orville? My doom, O Heaven—
But I'll retire to wear off this surprise,
And mould the phrase t' express my warring thoughts.

Col. Consent, I ask not; soon he will be here,
Give him an answer from thine own free heart.

SCENE SECOND—*Camp in the Woods, Captain's Quarters.*

CAPTAIN, *solus.*

So near the goal! O God, we praise thy name!
And when the great delivering deed is born,
Which now is struggling in the womb of Thought,
The ear of Heaven shall weary grow with song,
With the commingled shouts and anthems loud,
Of the delivered and the deliverers.
Oh, may the work be twin to the design;
And my conception, dark and lone as yet,
Within the silent chambers of the mind,
Take on the form of bright reality!
One bold and hearty stroke! I see the end:
Success already binds her laurel wreath
Around my brow, and blows the sounding trump
To celebrate the triumph of my plan.
From boyish days this hope has nourished me,

Else had I perished for the want of food:
For the spirit proud without the aim externe,
To call it forth into the world beyond,
Plays cannibal against its own dear self,
And with its own tooth gnaws the strings of Life.
This land shall be a land of freedom now,
Nor longer shall usurp a lying name,
Nor wear the painted harlot's gaudy visage,
Quite fair outside, but foulest filth at heart.
Then can I say I have a Fatherland,
Then shall I delight to bear its name;
But as it is, I spurn my native soil,
As devils do their brimstone bed of woe.
Rather had I be called a knave, a rogue,
Or epithet most villainous, than wear
The damning title of American.
My hate doth reach the unreasoning elements:
O Earth accursed, made for all mankind,
Yet seized, stolen, ravished by the few!
Thou hast been called by the fond name of mother,
'Tis not deserved, thou art unjust, unfair:
How can'st thou let a bondsman tread thy front?
He is a man too, spurn him as thou may'st.
Ye mountains, giants springing from the plain,
That grandly rise and threaten yonder sky,
Why hide ye not your lofty brows with shame
Or sink beneath to your primeval homes,
At view of this dire damned iniquity?
But higher still ye seem to raise your heads,
And smile from base to crown with moving green,
When ye should deluge all the plain with tears
Of molten snow or summit-dwelling clouds.
Yea, e'en this air so light in Northern climes,
Is heavy here, as if weighed down with chains,
And sympathetic with the burdened slave.
This land needs sore the purifier's hand,
And by the grace of God within these bounds,
A tempest of such fury shall I raise,
That this most foul and filthy stench of wrong
Shall all be cleansed away, and leave the air
As pure and sweet as on Creation's day.
Here from the distant hamlets of the North,
I've brought a few with zeal akin to mine;
These are my comrades in this enterprise;
A precious band who've bound themselves with me
In one unyielding bond of destiny,

With purpose to redeem the enthralled or die.

Enter HARWOOD.

Good even, Captain !

Capt.   Harwood, 'tis thou ?

Har.   Yes, but I do not wish to interrupt—

Capt.   Thou can'st not interrupt me—never ! Welcome !

Har.   But thou wert holding discourse with thyself
Upon some weighty point. Let me retire.

Capt.   Tush ! must I always coax and baby thee ?
Stay for my sake ! I have much on my heart
To tell thee of. Good Harwood, reach thy hand !
What thinkest thou ? Is not the prospect fair ?
Oh, Futurity ! Thy face shines like the sun !
I feel the crushing joy of hopes fulfilled,
The which, lifelong, have burned within my breast,
And found till now no egress for their flames.
To-morrow morning we shall be afield
Before the sun hath shot a single beam,
Reaping the harvest of Renown for us,
Of Right and Justice for the dark oppressed.
O haste your dragging pace, ye lazy Hours !
Your every moment seems Eternity
Cast in before my aim to thwart the deed.

Har.   Success ! for you, my friend, I hope the best.

Capt.   And why not for thyself ? Or has thy zeal
Which erst was glowing like the torch of day,
Burnt out to lifeless cinders and to dust ?

Har.   No look of mine e'er smiled upon this act.

Capt.   It is too late to croak disaster now.
Forebodings dark belong before the deed ;
Regret can not reverse the wheels of Time.

Har.   I sought to rein thy spirit, but in vain.

Capt.   The choice was free to thee to stay behind.

Har.   O friend ! thou know'st the throbbing of this heart
Beats time unto thy fortune and thy fate.
For I am so bound up in life with thee,
That though our reasons often be opposed,
Our wills are one and can not point apart.

Capt.   I make no charge against thy friendship's proof.
But lay this cankering fear aside, I pray,
Which makes thine arm fall nerveless at thy side,
When raised to strike the blow that tells thy fate.

Har.   What ! fear say'st thou ? No, 'tis impossible !
I thought thou knew'st me ! O ingratitude !
Sharp is thy tooth, and maddening thy sting !
A coward then, I am ? A pretty name

For one who ran away from peace and ease,
Forsook a loving mother's downy lap,
To save his life by hardship and by war.
Fear, thou art now my trembling pale-faced mate!
Though thee I falsely deemed my deadliest foe.
A sheer poltroon! A vile, knee-knocking knave!
Fear has become my dearest bosom friend:
For does he not dwell here within this breast?
Say rather, I am Fear and Fear is I.
Hear now a little story of this Fear:
There was a lovely boy whom scarce ten times
The earth had borne around her central orb;
His father's only hope, and pride and joy.
Alone he lay at night in thoughtless sleep:
A double tongue of fire leaped from his window,
In flaming garments soon the house was wrapped.
Who then did enter the red dragon's jaws,
From his devouring throat did tear thy child?
Fear, Fear it was, you say, for I am Fear.—
The fairest day was blooming of fair Spring;
Since then two years have passed the coming May;
A frenzied multitude dams up the streets,
And loads the air with shouts of "Hang the negro thief!'
Amid that raging, sweltering mass, I still can see
A cowering shape awaiting final doom.
One man darts quickly through the maddened throng,
He cuts the coil loose from the purpled neck,
And frees the gyved wrists, then fells in haste
Some two or three who try to stay the deed,
Bears *thee* away in triumph from the crowd,
To life and liberty, and to fresh air.
Who was he? ah! thou knowest him no more;
Then let me tell.   It was—this self-same Fear,
But for whose quaking hand and quivering heart,
Thy boy had been a heap of urnless ashes,
Thyself a stinking prey hung up for kites.
Oh then, henceforth, let me be titled Fear;
'Tis no disgrace to take his ugly name,
Who by so many deeds hath shown himself
A benefactor both to thee and thine,
And hence to me a benefactor too.

Capt.   Be calm! thou art my friend, I know it well,
Thy acts of kindness shall I ne'er forget.
But why so sharp and fiery are thy words?
Thy speech is like a red hot needle point,
Whose prick doth burn and still whose burn doth prick.

Upon thy courage would I cast no stain :
Thy gloominess alone I chid.

Har. The bravest soul hath oft presentiments,
And darkly views the fitful whims of chance.
'Tis not the danger to myself I fear ;
Within this scroll of flesh life loosely hangs ;
For any end of duty or of worth,
I'd fling it from me like a ragged mantle.
A friendly warning word I wish to speak :
To free the bondsman is a noble aim,
Well worth thy hand of steel and heart of fire ;
But it is good to scan in full the means,
Lest we pull down the world upon our heads,
And Sampson-like be buried 'neath the fall.
Beware ! to reach the goal of thy design,
Thou hast to travel o'er the nation's corpse,
Beat out thy Country's inner life, her laws,
Annul those sacred contracts of her birth,
Time-honored pledges, pacts and long good will,
Our anxious fathers' holy legacies.
Beware ! beware ! thou strikest at the State,
Whose right to live transcends the right of all.

Capt. The State indeed ! a figment of the mind,
To frighten fools and sway the multitude,
A cunning scheme by politicians framed,
For their own profit and the people's loss.
This hellish goblin hath possessed men's minds,
And made them stand aside and see the Right
Trodden beneath the master's iron heel.
The State has ever been the oppressor's friend,
And Freedom in her struggles with her foe,
Must never fear to strike, though he be clothed
In all the pompous vesture of authority.

Har. The fault with thee remains. For in our goodly State,
This virtue lies, that any citizen
May reach the highest rule by peaceful means :
First, bend to thine own mind the nation's will,
Then take the reins of power in thy hands ;
So, can st thou mould to beauteous life thy thought.

Capt. To please the multitude I ne'er was born,
Nor is't my wish. The barrier to my will,
Whatever it may be, I shall pull down,
And be a man untrammeled by the world,
For only thus my freedom is secure :
I, I, this individual, am supreme.
Thou hast consent to leave and go thy way.

Har.   Nay, nay, in spite of all that I have said,
          My heart is still the master of my action,
          And though the head rebels it clings to thee.

Capt. Well, let us thrust aside this aimless talk,
          Which hurts the quick fulfilment of our work,
          And feast upon the prospect of to-morrow.
          O glorious day, which brings the struggle keen,
          Yet sweeter to my soul than all the world,
          For thou shalt tow to port the freighted ship
          Of Hope, that hath till now been tossed at sea ;
          I would not barter for my previous life to-morrow.
          O Day ! that mak'st the radiant Sun thy heavenly bride,
          And cloth'st the joyous earth in shining garb,
          Bring with thee golden winged Victory,
          And in her gorgeous train, loud-chanting Fame,
          Nor shall a million throats of the Redeemed,
          Fail to join the universal shout of praise.

———

Scene Third—*De Harrison's Mansion.*

Clara, Edward, Col. De Harrison.

Col.   Here, Clara, is thy cousin ; know'st thou him ?
          He's come to greet his childhood's cherished mate,
          Who has so long been lost to him and me.

Cl.   What, Edward ? yes, 'tis so : marvelous growth !
          I left thee smooth in face, nor had'st thou passed
          As yet beyond the blooming goal of youth ;
          But now a bristly crop conceals the chin,
          And proudly tells the world : Here is a man.

Ed.   Nor has thy lore dried up thy juicy jests,
          Nor quenched in thee a loving maiden mind ;
          For beards are bird-lime to young ladies' eyes,
          Catching their glances first, and then their hearts.

Cl.   I see it well, thou art a trapper bold,
          Who knows his game and lays most cunning snares.

Ed.   And thou a wily fox that scents afar
          The huntsman's tricks, and fools the yelping hounds.
          —But let us stay this duel of our wits,
          And change it for the greeting sweet of friends
          And kindred that have long been separate.

Col.   Her long and grievous furlough has run out,
          Thank God ! and she is with us once again.
          Good nephew, say, has painter Youth not tinged
          His fairest rose upon my daughter's cheek ?

Ed.   To her more kind is Age than unto thee :
          Already has he furrowed deep thy front,

And bleached thy locks with never-melting frosts.
—Well Clara, dear, I'm pleased to see once more
Thy face lit up here in our sunny clime.
Long have I daily wished for thy return ;
I could not bear the thought that one I loved
Should dwell away from this her cloudless home,
In that most cheerless region of the globe.

Cl.   True, Nature here, has shown partiality ;
But *there* are beauties which *we* dream not of.

Ed.   Then have I lived to see the icy bear
Exalted o'er our starry crucifix,
And that too, by a daughter of the South.

Cl.   'Tis not the happy clime that makes the man,
Nay, rather say it unmakes more than makes ;
For wealth of Nature or of worldly goods
Doth ever rot what poverty doth rear.
Humanity for me hath greater charms
Than all the gorgeous tints the sun can paint.

Ed.   A sly and secret praise of Yankeedom !
That lying race of thieves unpunished ;
Whose only thought is cheat—whose God is gain.
But their deserts I wish not to conceal :
To them alone, belongs the glory great
Of decking knavery foul in robes of Heaven,
So fair, and pure, and holy does it seem.
One idol more they have : Hypocrisy ;
With veil so dark, and deep, and cunning-wrought,
That many wise men have been led astray,
To trust its lying oracles and shout
Through all this land "a God, behold a God ! "

Cl.   Methinks, dear cousin, that a Southern mist
O'erspreads thy mind and clouds thy reason's sun.
What some experience hath me taught of them,
I may declare to thee without offence :
The people there are great and good and free,
Attached to liberty and honest life ;
Firmly devoted to their fond ideas,
But yet sometimes intolerant to those
Who cannot see the world through their own eyes ;
Strong in belief, yet stronger in assertion,
And somewhat narrow in their wisdom, too ;
They take the greatest pains to know the right,
But knowing it they push it to extremes,
And often thrust it quite beyond itself,
So that its frail and beauteous form is lost.
One side of things they see both clear and deep,

And by no other people are surpassed ;
But the obverse side which is quite as real,
Lies ever hid beyond their vision's reach ;
As if the world might be a fastened coin,
With one face burnished, seen and read by all,
The other dark, eternally concealed ;
Thus all their greatness seems a mighty half.
To educate is there the highest end ;
Art, Science, Learning, find with them a home,
More generous patrons and ardent devotees,
Than elsewhere in our youthful land ; but still,
Their culture is a huge one-sidedness.
The people are, withal, great, good and free.

Col.   My daughter, this praise of thine seems overcharged.

Ed.   Cursed be the hireling varlets, cursed for aye !
It is a crouching, false and servile race ;
They load with fetters not the swarthy frame,
Not foreigners in blood, but their own kin ;
And sell in vilest servitude to gain,
It may not be their neighbors but themselves.
Their very name to me's the serpent's hiss.

Col.   Most true, my nephew, and most sharp thy speech.

Ed.   Their land, their clime, and their existence e'en,
I loathe ; my aim of life is them to hate ;
The soil on which they tread is tainted foul.
Scarce that direction can I turn my eye,
And rather had I Southward go to Hell,
Than through the North pass into Heaven's gates.

Cl.   Thy anger's quite amusing, Cousin dear,
So great excess must quickly sate itself ;
Thy wrath is like a shallow seething dish,
The more the heat the sooner is it dry.
But hear a gentle word from me, I pray :
Among that folk you deem so bad I've lived,
And shared their hospitality and care ;
How many friends of mine most true and dear,
Are in that distant clime, I need not say.
Their kindness seemed to me the dower of Heaven ;
A noble aim and spotless character
The spirits are that hover o'er the land ;
So must I speak a word in their defense.
Edward, methinks thou see'st some foggy shape,
Most huge and frightful, when beheld afar
In Northern sky, but quickly vanishing
When once the sun doth ray abroad his light.
Go live, eat, drink with them and know their life.

Col. No, no, enough it is thou hast been there;
    I fear I have in thee much to unteach.

Ed. Sooner would I take the Roman felon's fate,
    Be bagged with snakes and cast into the sea,
    Than housed one night within their viperous dens.

Cl. O tell me, whence has come this rancour fell,
    That bloats thy soul with poisonous vengeful speech,
    Transforms thy visage to a demon's look?

Ed. Turned Yankee, eh! turned traitress to thy land
    And blood! Such words as these are wont to hang
    Their hardy speaker on the nearest limb.

Cl. Be calm, and tell to me the grievances
    Whose thought now makes thy heart a bag of gall,
    And points thy tongue as sharp as adder's fang;
    Rehearse the cause of this most fearful hate,
    And all the facts with lawyer-like repose.

Ed. This inquiry appears to me most strange,
    When all the world doth see and shame our wrongs;
    Do they not hither come, t'entice away
    With secret lure, our slaves, our property?
    With what design, think ye? Philanthropy!
    To let them freeze and rot on British soil,
    Deprived of comfort and religious care.
    What venom is not spit upon the South?
    The Press, that monster of a thousand heads,
    Doth bellow daily from his thousand throats
    Most slanderous abuse of us and ours;
    Of our divine and patriarchal institution,
    Of our society and moral life;
    Emits into our land incitements bold,
    To conflagration, massacre, revolt;
    And e'en the holy ministers of Christ
    Stand ready with uplifted hands
    To bless the murderous deed. It is enough;
    I am prepared to soil my hands with blood,
    To wash our sullied honor of its stain,
    And to regain our Heaven-born rights.

Col. Though old, I'll take a musket in the cause,
    Pour out the dregs of my remaining life,
    To reach an end so high and dear to me,
    The more so, for my daughter is not mine.

Cl. O pardon me, my cousin and my father,
    My speech was rash, but meant not to offend.
    We have been very often wronged, I know,
    And should demand some satisfaction, too;
    But on the guilty let the burden fall,

> For of our rights we have there many friends,
> So do not lay on all the grievous charge.

Ed.   Nay, nay, methinks the guilt belongs to all.
> Would that the Atlantic with its watery plains,
> Was cast at once between ourselves and them.
> But that which cuts my heart into the core,
> Is their most foul, most base ingratitude;
> From products which we raise they have grown fat,
> And take their consequence among the nations;
> Without our commerce would their cities vast
> Lie waste with grass upon their thoroughfares,
> And only falling pillars mark the sites;
> Their most besotted masses rise and smite
> In hungry might the State and Property,
> And stretch to us their hands for food and work;
> All this they will not see, but serpent-like,
> They bite the breast that warms their limbs to life.

Cl.   A weighty case thou makest, I confess.

Ed.   Yet what is worst of all must now be told,
> Their duties in the federative bond
> Which joins in one our civil life and theirs,
> They have most basely shunned and shirked.
> And ta'en therein our choicest rights away.

Col.   Aye, sir, in that remark you hit the white,
> Their wanton acts we can no longer brook.

Cl.   'Tis true we have been sorely put to proof,
> Yet Patience never leaves the goodly soul
> But ever waxes with the growing need;
> Time will not always cast on us his frowns.

Ed.   That virtue I desire to be not mine,
> My wish, aye, my demand, is that we part;
> In peace untie the knot with careful hand,
> Or roughly cut it with the whetted sword.

Col.   My age would much perfer the former wise,
> But for the last could wield a heavy stroke;
> And my experience has not been so small;
> Upon the drilling ground, and in the camp,
> E'en on the battle field I've had my turn;
> For while a stripling still, to Florida
> I marched against the fierce red forester.

Cl.   You would not then disrupt the sacred bond
> Of State our Fathers joined with so much skill
> And anxious thought, and hoped to be eternal?

Col.   Aye, with a willingness that is not feigned.
> Agreement was the mother sole, we know,
> Of this confederation of the States;

And by agreement can it be dissolved.
Our greatest statesman showed the right long since,
And Right, though ne'er unsheathed retains its brightness;
With it the Will now locks its striving arms;
Where Right and Will join hands, the deed must follow.

Cl.   Men oft create what they dare not destroy.
The child's life hangs not on the parent's whim;
So too this State begot must live forever;
What right have ye to take a nation's life?

Ed.   The State has lost its end and is a curse,
No longer it protects our chartered rights,
But soon will smite us with its massive hand.
Its overthrow is now my highest hope,
So threatening look the omens in the North.
The reins which once we held in firmest grasp
Are being hourly twisted from our hands;
And soon the high-born sons of chivalry
Must bow the knee before mechanic lords.
Nay, that disgrace shall never stain our souls,
E'er long the entire South shall rise and show
The mighty majesty of wrathful honor,
Shall seize this often violated pact
Which chains her bosom pure to loathsome foes
And shall it rend into a thousand shreds.

ACT III.

Scene First.—*A Road.*

Enter Hoddle *and* Countryman *in the distance.*

Hod.   Here comes a native weed, I'll lay my head.
This rank, dank soil alone can bring such forth.
A very stalk of striding corn he comes.
Meet him I must.—I might avenge myself,
By telling now their plans and hiding-place,
And nip at once their budding enterprise;
But I shall not; for though they beat my flesh
Until it falls in black bits from my bones,
Treason ne'er shall force the entrance to my soul.
But wait! first shall I so confound this fellow,
By the juggle and displacement of fair words,
That he will not believe he is himself.

Co.   Good morrow, sir!

Hod.   Good morrow to yourself, sir!

Co.   Young man, thou seem'st a stranger in these parts.

Hod. Therein my seeming tells an honest tale ;
        Men often seem to be what they are not ;
        My seeming, so it seems, doth then not seem.

Co.   As full of seams thou art as any quilt ;
        Thou art a tailor, lad, if aught of trade,
        Is indicated by thy random talk.

Hod. Nay, nay, a doctor, if you wish to know ;
        For seeming, likewise, is the doctor's trade ;
        I come to purge with physic all of you.

Co.   That is a heavy dose for my belief.
        Where are thy pills and dark-compounded stuffs ?

Hod. Aye, they are lying ready for their work,
        Whene'er I bid them force their self-made way.

Co.   Thy speech is full of dark bewilderment,
        Or else I cannot understand thy tongue.
        Thou play'st with words as the unskilled at bowls,
        Not knowing where or how the ball may strike.
        Stranger, where is thy home, once more I ask ?

Hod. I am a Southron bold, of gentle blood,
        Who shuns dishonor's stain far more than Death.

Co.   In troth, thou art a funny, funny buck,
        I'd give a dozen ewes to know thy sire ;
        It was a rum old sod that nurtured thee.

Hod. Ha, ha, thou'rt right, quite right ; I am a sheep ;
        But mark ! should e'er I see thy face again,
        Thou'lt view a sheep which is not shorn, but shears.
        Longer, friend, I cannot tarry ; adieu !   *Exit.*

Co.   A damned mysterious dog ; his quiddities
        Are quite enough to break one's head with aches.
        I do not like him ; there is something wrong ;
        Such nonsense is by far too deep for fools.
        Let's see ;—"a sheep that is not shorn, but shears ; "
        That is, by his own word, a villain bold,
        Disguised beneath a modest mask ; 'tis so.
        Two weapons peered out their pocket's prison.
        As if their hard, dumb lips desired to speak,
        And send their small, round messengers,
        Like pills—I have it now ! I have in now !
        A Doctor? aye ! a veritable Doctor !
        The musket-ball is that most powerful pill,
        Which finds the shortest way unto the heart ;
        Such was the meaning couched beneath his cranks.
        How shied his words off from my questions' goal !
        And how uneasy was his look and tread !
        Then, too, that bunch of twigs he slyly held
        Within his grasp, what does it mean ?   I know ;

To set on fire our fences, houses, barns !
That is his dose of physic for us, I suppose.
There's somewhat in his looks that speaks of foul intent.
Follow I must ; I'll watch with stealth his steps,
And seek this serpent in his hidden nest.

SCENE SECOND.—*Another Road.*
Enter BUMBLE.

Bum. How glad am I t' escape their fiendish claws,
For fiends they are in all that makes the fiend,
And if they were soused down quite as they are,
Into the burning, brimstone element,
No one could tell them from the oldest demons.
These mad-caps would have slain me for a word
Spoke in discouragement of their wild hopes,
Because I was aweary of their game.
It was a cunning trick to slip so slyly off :
I thank you woods, for having hid my path,
Until it reached a point beyond pursuit.
Myself again ! I breathe more freely now,
Though they may iterate the whole day long,
This is a slavish soil and atmosphere ;
They are the slaves , I spit it in their faces,
That they do sorely need emancipation.
How clearly do I see in this sad strait,
'Tis not the outward bond that makes the slave,
But the base, narrow thought within the man.
A little vengeance now is in my power,
My sweat they shall repay with drops of blood,
'Twill give some solace to my ruffled soul ;
Their plans against this land I shall disclose,
And rouse the people to well-timed defence ;
Thus may I send them packing down to Hell.
Here is the dwelling which I came to sack,
But now it looks more friendly than my friends ;
It lends a screen 'gainst Heaven's burning eye ;
I must seek rest and shade or else I faint ;
Let fate bring what it may, I shall go in.

SCENE THIRD.—*Planter's Mansion.*
Enter BUMBLE.

Bum. Good morrow to this mansion's worthy lord !
I hope that I do not disturb his peace.

Pl.   Good morrow, enter and be welcome here.

Bum. I would but rest my wearied limbs awhile,
        And catch some draughts of shady air,
        Beneath this roof and bower of woven leaves.
        Old Sol has mounted to his highest throne,
        And rages like a tyrant o'er the world ;
        I am not wont to find him in so great a passion.

Pl.   Drink off this brimming bowl and slake thy thirst.

Bum. O water ! it is a draught the gods might grudge,
        If they are jealous, as is often said,
        To the dry and dusty throats of mortal men.

Pl.   Methinks another sun smiled on thy birth,
        Else our fierce, fiery charioteer of Heaven
        Would not appear to thee so great a stranger.

Bum. 'Tis true, my infant lungs breathed cooler air
        Than that which hovers o'er these hills and woods.

Pl.   I have transgressed, let me entreat thy pardon
        For my offence against thy privilege ;
        I did not mean t' inquire thy native soil.
        It was a goodly custom of the olden time,
        That hosts should never ask whence came the stranger
        Who lodged beneath their roof, but serve at once
        For him the choicest viands of their board ;
        Thus would I treat thee ; but my words had lapsed,
        E'er Reason clearly stamped them with her seal.

Bum. I am unworthy to receive these gifts ;
        They bring to mind a harsh comparison
        'Twixt thee and those on whom I have some claim.

Pl.   No claim for me is higher than the guest's ;
        My house is at your disposition sir.

Bum. Thy kindness cleaves the fetters of my tongue,
        And bids it speak the secrets of my heart.
        Listen ! I'll tell a story for thy good :
        Behind yon wood, and near the sea's broad arm,
        A band of men are hidden in the bush,
        Who threat destruction fell to thee and thine.

Pl.   Impossible ! whom have I so deeply wronged,
        That he should bring such woe upon my head ?
        Nay, thou dost only tell a dreadful tale,
        As seeming pay for hospitality.

Bum. Forgive, I pray, my crime—I must confess—
        I am of them, and have just left their camp ;
        I would no longer serve their bloody cause,
        And told them so ; then such a frenzy rose,
        That I could barely 'scape and bring my life.

Pl.   Who are they ? whence, with what design are come ?

Bum. From the far North they've sought this quiet coast,
As favorable to their plan ; they say,
With loud proclaim they come to free the slave,
And cool the people with a bath of blood.

Pl. Long has this bolt hung threatening in the clouds ;
Now has it lit upon our peaceful homes.
Quick, saddle me my steed ! no time for talk ;
I must in haste go seek our neighbors all,
And sound the sad alarm.   Come with me, boy.

SCENE FOURTH.—*The Camp.*

Enter CLARENCE, CAPTAIN, HARWOOD.

Capt. Now quickly to the bloody work my boys,
Each moment that we tarry on this spot,
Doth swell the hazard of our enterprise,
Until what once did seem a little hill,
Shall soon become a mountain in our way.
Two plans do show their outlines to mine eye,
And each makes weighty suit unto my will ;
But when the one I've ta'en, the other shows
So fair a face that I do me rue my choice.
Throw your advice into the doubtful scale,
And put a speedy end to this delay,
I beg, for restless time keeps spurring on.
Harwood and Clarence, give me your advice.
One plan is this: to rush forth from our lair
Like lions, seize our unsuspecting prey,
Where'er it may be found throughout this land ;
More cautious does the other counsel seem,
To spy out first the place and then to strike
Where 'tis the weakest, and for us the best.

Clar. My reason speaks most loudly for the last,
For if we shoot at random in the air,
We never hit, at most we fright our game,
Which being warned, flies off and warns the rest.
But let us first seek out the central point,
From which we safely can command this land,
Then dart like lightning forward to the deed.

Har. To this advice mine own opinion leans.

Capt. To your united wisdoms I shall yield.
But who shall take the hazard of this step ?
To this end hearken to my further thought :
Garbed as a simple wayfarer I'll go,
And give a stealthy look at every house

Which may be standing on our future road,
Survey each dubious nook in which a foe
Might lurk unseen, or else a friend could hide ;
Whisper the startling word of liberty,
Into the ear that hears but curses rude ;
Stir up strong arms to help us for themselves ;
Note the configuration of the land ;
In fine, select a spot by nature strong,
Which can be fortified still more by art,
Where we cán pitch our permanent abode,
Which may defy the most perverse attack.

Har. Nay, nay, dear captain, that will never do ;
Therein thy courage far outspans thy sense.
Thou know'st thou art the head of this grand work,
Which head once lost, the rest must perish too,
And we, thy followers, lie in one common grave.
I pray thee, let me go instead of thee !

Capt. Is not the peril as great to thee as me ?

Har. True, but my loss would be far less than thine.

Capt. The greatest danger should the chieftain seek.

Har. But think ! thou might'st be taken by the foe,
Then, with thy capture, captured are we all ;
As with thy death, we all are surely dead.

Capt. Play not such phantoms wild before thy mind.
How is it likely that I should be known
By people here, where I ne'er was before ?

Har. Some jealous accident doth strangle oft
The mightiest undertakings at their birth ;
Give chance no hold upon thy destiny.

Capt. Harwood, these monsters lie not in my path,
Nor can their grim look fright me from my will,
Else could I ne'er have reached these woody dales ;
And having thus defied Risk to his teeth,
Shall I now run before I see his face ?

Har. I see you do not understand the case ;
So shall I clothe my speech in plainest garb,
And show the reason of my importunity.
Hoddle returned a little while ago,
Whence he was sent by us ; he says he met
One man, a seeming rustic of the land,
But yet a man of dark, suspicious look.
They spoke and parted ; some little time gone by,
Our Hoddle turns about and sees this man
Following on his track ; 'twas not far hence.
Ere now he may have found our secret out,
And sown the news in every neighbor's ear ;

The which may soon bring forth upon our path,
A bristling crop of frowning enemies;
Or he may still be lurking in this brush,
And even listening to our counsel now.
Then do not go, the venture is too great.

Capt. No may-be can e'er turn me from my aim.
Thou playest with these possibilities,
Most like a little child with soapy bubbles,
Blowing them off his pipe of clay with glee,
To see them mount aloft and ride the air,
That seemeth jealous of their lightness bold,
And bursts to nought their watery rainbow film.
A pleasing sport for little folk, but 'tis
A craft unworthy of a man's estate.

Har. Then listen to this certainty I pray.
Bumble has left our camp in secret wrath.
No one has seen him since he stole away;
He has, no doubt, deserted to the foe.

Capt. Ha, ha! this is not certain still, my boy;—
But it is startling news! The Devil's imp!
Indeed he has fulfilled my highest hopes;
For treachery was written in his down-cast eyes.
Perchance 'twere best to take our other plan.

Har. Better by far than that thou go'st, methinks.
Thy duty bids thee stay upon this spot.

Clar. Captain, 'tis so; thou should'st remain with these;
But list a moment to my own request:
I have a plan to solve this knotty point;
I offer here to go myself, and bring
All information which you say you need.
Before the sun hath sped through half the orb
Which yet remains to him ere day is done,
I shall return. Till then a patient soul
Possess ye all.

Capt. Well said, go, Clarence, dear;
In thee I have almost as much of faith
As in myself, which is not small, thou know'st.

————

Scene Fifth.—*Near DeHarrison's Mansion.—Evening.*

Enter D'Orville *and* Edward DeHarrison.

Ed. D'Orville, hast thou yet seen my cousin Clara,
And spoke to her about that nice affair?

D'Or. Ah, I have had that sweet delight and pain.

Ed. Why, thou art in a melancholy trim:

Make not wry faces at so bright a sun,
Thou cans't not put his fervid splendor down.

D'Or. I see no sun, a cloud hangs o'er my soul,
And darkly crapes the Future like a bier.

Ed. Tut, courage, man, thy suit is not yet lost.

D'Or. Hope is not drowned, but labors in a sea
In which the waves dash oft above her head;
Such furious tempest she can't long withstand.

Ed. Oh, pipe no more this sickly strain, I pray!
It makes an ugly blot on manhood's page.
Now tell the facts about your interview;
I can, perchance, help thee in this rugged way.

D'Or. Hear then, a story of endeavor vain.
I sought t'engage her in a little talk,
About the lands and people she had seen;
And then t'approach some tender theme,
That might serve as an outlet to my soul;
This were the Cupid-winged ship whereon
I thus might sail into love's happy port;
But she, as cognizant of my design,
Did alway subtly shy the looming point,
And ran abroad to other things remote;
Most cleverly she played these shirking cranks.
Two weary hours she circled round and round.
And I in hot pursuit sped for the prize,
When I by the long race became fatigued,
And so gave up the agonizing chase.

Ed. Ha, ha! that was a royal hunt in troth.

D'Or. But stop! here comes a stranger on our path.

[*Enter* CLARENCE *disguised as a pedestrian.*]

Clar. May I disturb awhile your eager talk?—
How far is it to the nearest hamlet, pray?

Ed. Ascend yon little knoll, beyond the wood
It dots the hill-side sloping to the vale;
Soon you will see the houses; just go on.

Clar. Will you be pleased to tell its name, I beg?

Ed. Assuredly! 'tis called Palmettotown.

Clar. Ha, yes! I know that name, Palmetto town,
I've heard of it before—Palmetto town—
I'm glad I am so near Palmetto town.
[*Aside.*] Within the radius of a furlong hence
She lives, whose magnet draws me from the pole.

Ed. What sudden joy doth try to burst thy heart,
Dost thou return home after absence long?

Clar. Nay, sir, not *that.* But tell me, if you will,
What old majestic mansion 'mong the trees

Doth yonder sleep, o'er which the aged oaks
Stand sentinel with loving, watchful look?

D'Or. It bears a name of highest rank and worth,
A name nobility might wear with grace,
If 'twere the custom here—DeHarrison.

Clar. Heavens! DeHarrison! in yonder house!
Fortune, smile on! Indeed, so soon! so near!
Young man, thy eulogy gives out much warmth.—
Oh, pardon me, it is not far from town,
You say—just let me see—yes, so it is.
The day begins to yawn, and now hath stretched
The drowsy cap of night upon his head;
I would not wish to find myself alone
Upon these woody paths without the sun.
Your pardon, gentlemen, I must be off.

Ed. God save you from all shadows dire; good night. *Exit Clar.*

D'Or. He seems to know, yet not to know this spot.

Ed. A passing stranger who the village seeks.

D'Or. Yet how he startled at thy family's name;
And then his joy he sought to hide 'neath words.

Ed. It is not worth the talk.—Here we must part;
The dew hath moistened now the thirsty earth,
Whose face the whole day long the sun did scorch;
And now the grass doth wash the dusty feet
Of passing swains with its wet store of wealth.
D'Orville, courage! 'tis my last word to-night;
Not the weak heart should hamper the wise will.
Good night.

D'Or. Farewell! I'll see thee soon again.   *Exit Edward.*
Where shall I go, now that I am alone?
Alas! the heaviest load that burdens men
Is but themselves;—I'd hurl this hateful pack
From me, yet, ah, this hateful pack is—I.
If I could only rid me of myself,
It were a happiness; but 'tis self-murder,
And that's a monster, from which mankind recoils.—
What raging fires are kindled in my flesh
Which make the fountain of my blood so seethe?
Is molten iron running through my veins?
O heaven! water! I am burning up!
My heart has now become a funeral pile
Whereon I am both offering and offered.
I wish I were a thousand miles away!
Hold, foolish wish, let me recall thee quick;
It were most mad to go, I'd soon return.
No longer, ah! do I possess myself,

My highest freedom has become a slave.
I wish to God I ne'er had seen her face !
O, no ! the very fancy drives me mad,
I cannot think of my existence here
Apart from her ; it were a chill blank waste ;
I would impale my life upon my dirk.
I must turn back, and once again to-night
Her form I must behold ; that view alone
Can slake the soul-consuming thirst of Love.
It is her wont to pace her garden late,
Some hidden overlooking spot I'll find,
And with the friendly aid of this bright moon
I shall feast full my eyes with that fair sight.

Scene Sixth.—*Night.*

Enter Planters *with* Bumble *before the house of De Harrison.*

1st Pl. Ho, rouse this house, up, sleep no more,
  Till you can sleep beneath the wings of peace ;
  The sword of danger swings above your heads.
2d Pl. Hallo ! Awake, De Harrison, awake !
  Murderers, robbers, thieves, are nigh ! Hallo !
  Come, help us, quickly, else we all are lost.
   [Col. DeHarrison *appears above* at a window.]
Col. Here am I ! What's the matter ? Who are ye ?
  Wherefore have ye come here to fright away
  The timorous wings of sleep from our abode ?
3d Pl. Thou knowest us, thy neighbors are we all ;
  Come forth, we have some news to roil thy blood.
  A villainous gang of cut-throats from the North
  Have landed on our shores to steal our slaves,
  Destroy our property, o'erturn our State ;
  We wish to rouse the villagers to arms,
  Come down, thou wast a soldier, head our band.
Col. 'Tis strange ! Wait, in a moment I am there.
1st Pl. How fair the moon smiles on these bloody works !
2d Pl. Methinks she ought to veil her face with clouds.
3d Pl. Young man, you say you can lead to the spot.
Bum. Aye, just where they are lying in the woods.
  'Tis straight upon this road above the corners.
Col. [*comes out.*] What certain proof have ye of this foray ?
1st Pl. Here's the youth, of their own number, too,
  Who's told the entire story of their plan.
   Countryman *enters running.*
Co. Arm quickly all this crowd ! Why stand ye here
  While your destruction nears ? Seize first what lies

Upon your path to wield against attack;
An enemy lies in yon woods ensconsed
Ready to pounce upon his thoughtless prey.

Col. What ground have ye for all this heavy news?

Co. I saw a stranger of suspicious mien
Upon the road; we spoke—his words were dark,
As if he would conceal some fell design;
And so I followed him to find it out.
I tracked him quickly to a woody lair,
And hid me in the bush and heard their counsel,
To-morrow with the lark they will march forth.

Col. Then follow me; to-night we shall prepare [*except Bumble.*
To meet them with their own foul terms of force. *Exeunt all*

Bum. These fellows are too hot for my cool blood,
I think I'd better turn another road,
For on this one I see but broken heads. *Runs off.*

Scene Seventh.

Enter CLARENCE *in the vicinity of DeHarrison's mansion.*

Clar. The house is darkened and in deep repose.
Let my dear birdie sleep till morn appears,
Then shall the shining shield of Phœbus smite
The drowsy world and bring in life again,
His beaming fingers gently ope her eyes.
Heaven forefend her slumber be disturbed!
Noise in this holy calm were sacrilege;
Hence, silent shall I bide the coming sun.
Beneath the bushes and the clambering vines
Which hug this garden-wall of mossy stone,
Forming a shadow which forbids each glance
To penetrate its secret bosom dark,
I shall dispose myself for tranquil rest,
And listen to the stillness of the sacred night;
For solitude doth often tinkle in the air.
Shine on, Diana fair, thou huntress bold,
That daily put'st to rout the boastful sun,
Be thou the sweet companion of my watch;
Let fall thy silvery hair from thy bright head,
And fill the sleeping earth with quiet light,
Until thy greater brother whips his steeds
From out the sea, and mounts with hasty stride
The eastern convex of the globous sky,
Bringing captive morn chained to his chariot-wheels.
[CLARA *enters the garden.*]

Cl. What fearful rumors ride upon the air,

To fright away the beauty of this night !
Heaven protect my father from all harm.

Clar. [*Aside*] Methinks I hear a voice within this wall.

Cl.   How silent and majestic is the hour !
The wind, aweary of her bootless wail,
Doth lay herself and sleep with mortal men ;
The moon hath burnished brightly every star
That shimmers in her nightly trail of blue,
As she most queenly sweeps along the sky ;
But ah, the heart shares not dull nature's rest,
This lull has brought a storm to many a soul.

Clar. [*Aside*] Is this a spirit prisoned here that dares
To tell its sorrows only to the Night ?

Cl.   The time I last did catch his winsome look,
Blooms forth the fairest flower of Memory.

Clar. [*Aside*] Or is't a maid bewailing to the moon
Her absent lover and her loved griefs ?
I'll list again, for I would gladly hear
Such plaints about myself upon this spot.

Cl.   [*Nears*] Oh were my soul disrobed of grievous clay,
And set afloat to mingle with the clouds,
I'd fly at once to his far Northern home,
And hovering o'er him as he lies in sleep,
I'd speak to him in dreams, and tell my love :
In ringlets round I'd wreathe his heavy hair,
And plant a kiss on every bit of lips,
That he would say, methinks, when he awoke,
The fairy-queen had wooed him all that night.

Clar. [*Aside*] A most sweet fantasy ! I must see, too ;
Hearing is not enough for such fair words.

Cl.   Oh, Clarence, Clarence, why art thou so far ?
Already our two names are married quite,
Why should our hearts by space be torn asunder ?

Clar. [*Aside*] 'Tis she, 'tis she, by Heaven, and me she means !

Cl.   Oh would that thou wert here, sweet love, with me,
To walk among these flowers and smell their breath,
Conversing all the while about the time
When first we read our fate in each other's eyes ;
Then we would sit us down and watch the moon,
And thus would whisper low our mutual love.

Clar. Accursed wall, thou shalt not bar me out,
I'd mount thy back tho' it did reach the skies.   *Leaps over.*

Cl.   What sudden shape here rises on my dreams !
Help ! help ! O, holy Father, save thy child !

[CLARENCE *throws off his disguise, appears armed and kneels.*]

Clar. O, noble maid, thou hast no cause for prayer ;

At thy most gracious bidding here am I.
Oh! stay thy frightened pace awhile and list,
I am that Clarence, whom thou just didst call.
    [D'ORVILLE *rushes from the opposite side and draws.*]

D'Or. Most villainous of caitiffs, stand, I bid!
This action here thou must make good by arms.
It is a deed of which the Devil were ashamed,
Thus to waylay an unprotected maid.
I'll tap thy coward heart and draw its blood,
That ne'er again thou wilt disgrace thyself,
And so I shall befriend thee 'gainst thy will.
Defend thyself! I would not steal thy blood.
      [CLARENCE *draws, they cross swords.*]

Cl. Oh, God, 'tis he! [*rushes between*] Clarence put up thy blade,
I would not have thee stain its pure chaste glow,
Its brightness e'en a drop of guilty blood would soil.

Clar. How can I disobey thy first command?
I shall, sweet love, although the mind rebels:
My sword was never drawn before in vain.

Cl. O tell me, who has brought thee to this spot?
Thou'rt fallen from Heaven in answer to my prayer,
For thee my daily orisons have long been raised;
Dear Clarence, is this not a happy dream?
Think me not bold, I've heard thee call me love,
Then let me, too, unveil my ready heart,
And call thee by the thousand names of love.—
But, whence this hateful contrast of a man,
That shadow-like doth follow thy dear frame
And blights our presence here and our free tongues?
Fortune, thou art thine own self's contradiction,
Uniting the most loved with the most loathed!
D'Orville, sheathe now thy eager sword, and tell
Why thou profanest thus my privacy?

D'Or. Most humble pardon must I beg of thee,
For this bold, seeming-rude intrusion here;
But weigh my motive ere I may be judged.
As I did lie beneath yon orange-tree,
My fancy feeding on sweet thoughts of thee,
I saw thy form pass through this garden-gate
And heard thee holding converse with thyself,
When suddenly this fellow scaled the wall,
As if to pluck thee off against thy will,
Or work some horrid shame on thy fair frame;
Then thy unsullied life I thought to save
By casting mine before dark danger's tread.

Cl. D'Orville, for this most gallant act of thine,

To give thee have I naught but grateful thanks;
It is a poor return for thy good will;
And if I had two hearts within this breast,
One shouldst thou have, so worthy is thy deed;
But the sad single heart, which pulses here,
Is mine no more to grant away to thee;
It hath ta'en lodgement in another's breast,
And would not for the world forsake its home.

D' Or. Thou dost not mean this man?

Cl.   Aye, him I mean.

D'Or. Adieu, I shall not mar your happy hours. *Exit D'Orville.*

Cl.   How joyous 'tis to peer into thine eyes,
And see the rippling smiles run o'er thy face,
By the faint silent light of yonder orb.

Clar. More joyous still it it to press thy hand
In mine, and feel the fierce magnetic fire
Dart through my frame, like lightning in the clouds;
And then to lay thee softly to my breast,
And hear the secret throbbing of thy heart.

Cl.   Sweet Clarence, say, how hast thou hither come?

Clar. O stranger, stranger that the wildest dream!
But tell me first, dost thou requite my love?

Cl.   My chamber nightly did I fill with sobs,
My eyes held brimming tears at thought of thee,
For it so seemed I ne'er would see thee more,
And so my soul was always seeking hard
To quit this hateful flesh, and fly away.

Clar. O what delight doth snatch my struggling breath,
And choke me with a multitude of sweets!
This moment 's the quintessence of my life!
What happiness to win the golden prize!
Thou art a radiant angel of the sky,
I feel unworthy of thy noble worth;
Can it be so, art thou then here with me,
And dost give back brim full my cup of love?
Or is it one of Night's fair pleasing cheats?
Vouchsafe thy milky hand to my hot lips,
To quench awhile their parching thirst of love.

Cl.   Clarence, be calm; we'll talk no more of love,
But let our actions to our hearts be tongue.
Now answer, dear, what I before did ask,
How did'st thou come to find my nightly haunt?

Clar. Oh yes, wake me from this bright paradise,
It is too much delight to long endure;
I have ill news to mingle with these joys.—
From the far North I've tracked the wayless main

To warn thee of th' impending hour of woe;
A band of men conspire against the homes
Of thy dear father and thy neighbors here;
Not far away from this fair spot they lie.
I am an officer of high command
And weighty trust; wherefore you see me here,
Dispatched by them to seek th' attacking point.

Cl.   Nay, Clarence, nay, this is not so, methinks;
You do but jest, you will but frighten me,
To make my future happiness more keen.

Clar.   In most sad earnestness I speak to thee.

Cl.   Oh, what a sudden cloud bedims my sun!
Could not some peaceful way have led thee here?
Then were our joy unspotted with a sigh;
Such ugly wings ne'er brought so bright a blessing.
I fain would curse the means, but then I think
What precious freight was thus to me conveyed,
And so I'm torn by gladness and by grief.
Clarence, say once more and then I shall believe;
Art thou in arms against my native land?

Clar.   My body is in seeming armor wrapped,
But still my soul doth seek a peaceful aim
To rescue thee and thine from War's fierce look.
Flee quickly, with thee bear what well thou can'st
Of goods and jewels rare, but most thyself;
Wake up the household, and take all along;
Warn thy old father of this sudden danger;
Remain until the storm has passed these skies;
Methinks its rage will very soon be spent.

Cl.   Mine only jewel in the world art thou,
Thee would I take along and safely keep.

Clar.   That blissful time can not now be for us,
I quickly must return, my time is out.

Cl.   Thou wilt not leave me here alone to fight
The shadows fell of fancy in the dark?

Clar.   Doth no one dwell within the house but thee?

Cl.   My father has gone out to meet the foe.

Clar.   What, is this expedition known to you?

Cl.   A band of men left here some time ago
To summon all the neighborhood to war;
They chose my father captain of their troop.
I pray, lift not your hand 'gainst his gray hairs.

Clar.   Nay, nay;—then must I go and tell our men
To scatter to the winds ere they are caught,
For treason has divulged their whole design.
A parting kiss, dear Clara, and I am off.

Cl. O heaven! this affray bodes me much ill.

Clar. Nay, love, our stars shall join us soon again.
Adieu.

———

SCENE EIGHTH—*Camp.*

CAPTAIN, HARWOOD, SERGEANT.

Capt. Sergeant, see if the men are ready soon;
The morn is now upon our perilous path,
And shows us to the eyes of all the world;
The deed is waiting for our quick decision.   *Exit Sergeant.*

Har. It is most strange that Clarence comes not back;
Some hours have passed since that he should be here.

Capt. An accident may have seized him on his way.

Har. It can not be that treason taints his heart.

Capt. Thou hast no evidence of such intent?

Har. No.   Still I thought his 'haviour often strange.

Capt. Harwood, again thou art at thy old game;
Of dark surmises is thy head as full
As is the bristly porcupine of quills,
Which thou dart'st forth with every tick of time,
To sting with doubt the purposes of men.
Away with all long-faced conjecture now,
I shall not hear it, I am off to work.
Enter SERGEANT.

Ser. Here are the men prepared for thy commands.

Capt. Well done, my comrades dear, at such fair hour
To be in trim for this long day's hot work;
It shows your zeal in our most holy cause,
Beyond all power of rhetoric or oath.
Are ye all ready for the fight?

All.   Aye, aye.

Capt. To free the bondsman, or else let the grass
Upon these fields be both your winding-sheet
And your uncoffined graves.

All.   So may it be.

Capt. Then but a word of counsel have I left:
Keep e'er this bending feather in your eyes,
Whose snowy whiteness doth embrace my head.
Enter SENTINEL.

Sen. The foe, the foe!

Capt.   What dost thou say?

Sen. A band of armed men are bearing for this spot.

Capt. O happy, holy hour!   Good sentinel!
Thou bringest joyful news!   Now to the work!

And with the shout of Freedom on our lips,
Whose echo shall break every servile chain
Throughout this land and strike oppressors mute,
At them, my braves !   *They all rush out.*

Scene Ninth.

Enter Col. DeHarrison *and* Band.

Col. Halt ! yonder are the woods, the traitorous woods,
Which hide within their breast our enemy ;
I shall not long delay your eager hearts ;
Remember in this struggle that ye fight
For homes, wives, children, and your honor too.
        Clarence *enters at a little distance.*

Clar. What ! these are not my friends, I must retreat.
        D'Orville *enters.*

D'Or. Halt ! rabbit-hearted caitiff, thee I know ;
Thou art a craven spy, unsheathe thy blade ;
We'll end th' encounter which we once began.

Clar. My sword I'll prove more ready than my tongue,
And thou, God willing, shalt answer with thy life,
For thy vile, slanderous speech.   *They fight.*

D'Or. I'm slain, I'm slain, my blood shall be avenged !
Help ! hither friends, vengeance !
        Enter Edward DeHarrison *with several men.*

Ed.   Whose cry is this ?
Upon my soul, 'tis D'Orville, my dear friend ;
Sir, what means this bloody deed ?

Clar.   I was assailed.

Ed. Ha, ha ! I recognize thee now ; thou art
A spy, assassin, villain ; die on this spot.   *Stabs him.*

Clar. O God, my heart is pierced, this is my end ;
Farewell, sweet earth, I leave thee not with joy,
For on thy front my fairest Clara treads ;
My parting word I scarcely shall fulfill.
        Captain *enters with his band.*

Capt. What shape is this ? our Clarence, by the gods !
O wretch, art thou the author of this deed ?

Ed. Worm, viper, Devil, I am, and 'tis my boast.
Come on, thou fiend, I'll hack to gobbets thee
And all thy damned crew, and strew your flesh
To carrion kites and dogs.   How dare ye stamp
Your hellish tracks upon our sacred soil ?

Capt. Slave-monger, go fright thy slaves with empty threats,
Not men ; I'll cut a mouth within thy heart,

That it may speak its venom quickly out.
Set to.   *They fight, Edward is run through.*

Ed.   Alack! So soon the strings of life are cut.

Capt. Push on, my men, and sweep them from the field.
                    [*The other side retreats.*]

Col. Stay, hold, here is fresh succor for us now;
Rush for them, and we'll turn this surging tide.—
So; once again; one more fierce dash, they fly.

Capt. Old man, the stoutest heart of all thy band
Thou hast; go back, or else thy hoary head
Shall tumble from thy shoulders 'neath this edge.

Col. My age demands no mercy at thy hands;
I have at thee.

Capt.   Thou rash old fool, take that!

All. Vengeance! DeHarrison is slain! Vengeance!   [*Captain.*
    [*The Captain's party retreats. A rush is made toward the*

Capt. Six rival steeled points at once! I die;
But ah, than death more bitter is the thought,
My aim with me doth perish on this spot.—
Nay, it shall not, it hath an eternal germ,
Which fertile Time shall nurse and yet mature;
Some luckier hand shall execute this plan,
Or e'en a nation arm itself with my design.

                    CLARA *enters.*

Cl. What fearful sights are scattered o'er this plain!
I would return, but no, I am pushed on,
For I must know my fate in this day's strife.
Whose form is this? It is my cousin Edward!
A hardy soul that bravely gave itself away.
O that I could stay by thy side, and wash
Thy body with my tears, but on I must.—
Ah, whose white hairs are these? My father's, oh!
Great God! why hast thou not ta'en me along;
Let me once kiss to life these lips and brow;
Thy looks are fierce as cast upon the foe;—
Nay, nay, they're tender, loving as my father's.
Thy seeless eyes, oh gently let me close.
My father's shade, forgive ingratitude;
I must another face now seek with haste,
If it should chance lie on this bloody field.—
This is D'Orville, a bold and gallant youth,
And near him here—O Clarence, Clarence—dead!
Thou'rt gone, thou'rt flown, and borne with thee my life!
The dagger which did pierce thy manly breast
Hath reached my heart.   *Sinks.*

Enter HARWOOD.

Har.   Such is the fearful end of this foray.
         I have foreseen it long, for violence
         Must ever turn upon itself at last,
         And be destroyed by its own bloody hand.
         Captain, sleep well, a dauntless mind thou had'st,
         A soul, which, when it once conceived an aim,
         Without delay must give it birth in deed ;
         This was the cursed bane that brought thee here.
         Now, nought to me remains but to the dead
         To pay the final rites, collect the few
         Who yet remain and leave this fatal soil.

THE END.

www.ingramcontent.com/pod-product-compliance
Lightning Source LLC
Chambersburg PA
CBHW021238260626
47172CB00002B/829